CHEERS FOR A
DOZEN
EARS
A SUMMER CROP OF COUNTING

Felicia Sanzari Chernesky

Illustrated by **Susan Swan**

Summer Squash is here!

fresh fresh fresh Corn

just picked Tomatoes

fresh Blueberries it's time for a Picnic!

Beat the Heat! Cold Cold Cold Watermelon

Albert Whitman & Company
Chicago, Illinois

Dog day August

and it's steamy hot.

Let's take a drive to
the farm stand spot.

Bring Mom's list so we don't forget
these fruits and veggies. Ready? You bet!

1 watermelon so smooth and round.

2 purple eggplants
that weigh two pounds.

3 bell peppers: orange, green, and yellow.

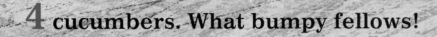

4 cucumbers. What bumpy fellows!

5 silly squashes that make us laugh.

6 berry boxes!
(Mom puts back half...)

7 stinky onions to slice and cry.

8 fuzzy peaches for homemade pie.

9 fine tomatoes
are firm and red.

10 plump plums
will keep us well-fed.

11 green beans—not one bean more.
Moms adds a bunch.
(What'd she do that for?)

12 o'clock hungry. We're almost done.
Choose a dozen ears of fresh-picked corn.

Wildflower
HONEY

our very special
Peach
JAM

vine ripened
TOMATOES

Now we have each item on Mom's list.
Wait! Here's one more we can't resist.

Add a summer sunflower from the jar.
Now let's take this garden to our car!

But first, put some money in the can.
Farmers work hard to feed this land.

We've counted up
the list we made.
Now let's head home
and find some shade!

For Mom—who taught us to pick plum tomatoes and count Jersey corn blessings.—FSC

For Celisse, Zane, Alex, Roarke, Kendall, and Morgan.—SS

Library of Congress Cataloging-in-Publication Data
is available from the publisher.

Text copyright © 2014 by Felicia Sanzari Chernesky.
Illustrations copyright © 2014 by Susan Swan.
Published in 2014 by Albert Whitman & Company.
ISBN 978-0-8075-1130-5

Printed in China.
10 9 8 7 6 5 4 3 2 1 BP 18 17 16 15 14 13

For information about Albert Whitman & Company,
visit our web site at www.albertwhitman.com.